31974

Titles in the series:

BREAK JENNIFER LANE	**ME²** CATHERINE BRUTON
DELETE TIM COLLINS	**OUT!** IAIN McLAUGHLIN
FINAL GIRL TIM COLLINS	**PARADISE** TIM COLLINS
HAVE A GO JON MAYHEW	**PLAGUE** ECHO FREER
IN THE STARS ECHO FREER	**RUNAWAY** ANN EVANS
KEEPER ANN EVANS	**S/HE** CATHERINE BRUTON
KILL ORDER DANIEL BLYTHE	**THE CRAVING** CLIFF McNISH
LAST YEAR IAIN McLAUGHLIN	**WASTED** KAREN MONCRIEFFE

Badger Publishing Limited, Oldmedow Road, Hardwick Industrial Estate, King's Lynn PE30 4JJ

Telephone: 01438 791037

www.badgerlearning.co.uk

ME²

CATHERINE BRUTON

ME² ISBN 978-1-78837-196-4

Publisher: Susan Ross
Senior Editor: Danny Pearson
Editorial Coordinator: Claire Morgan
Copyeditor: Cheryl Lanyon
Designer: Bigtop Design Ltd
Cover: © Noa Salti / Alamy Stock Photo

2 4 6 8 10 9 7 5 3

CHAPTER 1
SUMMER SUN

Molly wasn't sure how long she'd been staring at the same page. The summer sun streaming across her desk made the letters on the white paper dance and swirl. She blinked hard, tried to force herself to concentrate, but the muddle refused to shape into words.

Molly sighed. Her head ached and the neon numbers on the desk clock glared at her: 11.47am. Had she really been sitting here for nearly three hours? She was already way behind on her revision schedule — carefully colour-coded, tightly timed, each hour plotted and allotted to a different subject. It had felt so safe, so ordered. It had made her feel in control in the chaos that had descended on the family after Mum…

"Dad, I'm going to the launderette." Molly pushed back her chair quickly, sending a pile of revision notes fluttering across the floor.

The washing machine had been on the blink for a week. Dad had promised to get someone to fix it but he hadn't. Molly shoved some dirty clothes into a bin bag and made her way downstairs.

"I'll pick up some food for supper, OK?"

No reply.

She glanced into the lounge where Dad was sitting staring at the TV, still in his pyjamas, unshaven, eyes glassy.

He didn't seem to have heard.

He didn't even notice when she let herself out of the front door.

Would he notice if she never came back?

Like Mum.

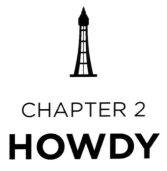

CHAPTER 2
HOWDY

Molly made her way through the streets
to the launderette. You could just see the beach
from here, smell the chips and candyfloss from the
promenade, hear the tunes from the arcades, the
braying of donkeys on the pebbles. But away from
the glitz of the seafront, Blackpool was just like
any other town — sort of.

Molly had brought her revision notes but she
found herself staring at her own reflection in
the washing machine — pale face, mousy hair
pulled into a messy ponytail, faded blue eyes.
Like Mum's.

Then she realised she was staring into a different set of eyes. A girl was sitting behind her — her reflection laid over Molly's so their gaze met in the swirling reflections of pants, socks and shirts.

"Howdy, stranger!"

Molly turned. The girl was perched on top of one of the drying machines, brown legs swinging in time to the radio. She was Molly's age — dressed sort of the same but also totally different. Her shirt was unbuttoned and tied at the waist to show off her slim brown midriff. Her jeans were full of rips, her hair in a jaunty side ponytail, smudges of dark eyeliner ringing intense blue eyes. At her neck she wore a heart-shaped locket that reminded Molly of one Mum used to wear.

"I'm KT," said the girl. "Spelled K–T, not the boring way. Please don't tell me you're revising!"

"Sort of," replied Molly.

"I totally should be too. But study leave sucks. The sun is shining — and we are cooped up inside learning dates and quotes? It's child cruelty."

Molly found herself smiling.

"So — Molly — that's your name?"

The girl called KT — spelled the cool way — was staring at the notes with Molly Cairns neatly written on each page.

"So, Molly, shall we get out of here? Ditch the studying? Go to the Pleasure Beach?"

Molly didn't know what to say. "Um, what about the washing?"

KT laughed — a little too loud. The old lady behind the counter glanced over with a frown.

"Live a little, Molly!" KT jumped off the machine. "Come into the sunshine, MC. All work and no play makes Molly a dull, dull girl!"

CHAPTER 3
KT

Molly wasn't sure why she followed her. Maybe it was the sun. Or the laughter in KT's eyes. The brain-frazzling revision, the gut-wrenching ache of Mum. After all, she deserved a break. And before she knew it they were both running out of the launderette grinning, KT yelling, "We'll pay when we pick up!"

Then they were down on the promenade with the holiday crowd, running past the crazy horse-drawn Cinderella coaches, past stalls selling fried doughnuts and rock in every colour of the rainbow. Dashing helter-skelter along the seafront, the smell of stale beer, vomit and cigarettes thick in the summer air. Past the pier and the aquarium till they arrived at the gates of the funfair, breathless and laughing.

Before Mum got ill, Molly loved the Pleasure Beach. She loved riding on the Teacups and the Alice in Wonderland ride. There was a picture of Mum, Dad and Molly on the Log Flume — wet and shrieking. That was the summer before Mum was diagnosed. When the sun was always shining and Molly hadn't heard of words like lymphoma and chemotherapy.

"So, hand it over, Molls."

"What?"

KT was grinning at her. "We need to pay for tickets to ride, kiddo."

"I've only got the launderette money."

"Perfect!" KT grabbed Molly's purse, handed a note to the bored-looking girl behind the till.

"But…"

"Molly, no one lies on their deathbed worrying about the laundry!" said KT, giving her a look. "Right?"

Suddenly the smell of sea-salt mixed with stale grease and candyfloss made memories flood back. A family walked past. The mother and father were swinging the little girl up into the air: "One, two, three… wheee!"

Molly blinked away the memories, plastered a fake grin on her face and said, "OK — bring it on!"

CHAPTER 4
ARCADE

KT wanted to go on all the rides. The faster and louder the better. She was a total thrill junky, and it wasn't just the rollercoasters.

"Dare you to steal one of those sugar dummies," she said as they went past a stall selling rock and candyfloss.

"KT, you are insane!" said Molly, but she was giggling. She felt high on the heat of the day. KT's wild energy was infectious.

"If you are too chicken, I will!"

And then KT was darting towards the stall. The attendant was busy with a group of tourists. KT winked at Molly, grabbed a dummy, and they ran for it.

They collapsed, panting with laughter, by the arcade. The smell of fried fish from a nearby stall made Molly realise she hadn't eaten all day.

"Won't your parents be worried?" she asked KT.

"Doubt it," said KT. She'd told Molly they'd recently moved from London. Her parents weren't around much. "Your turn!"

"No way!"

"Listen, I rescued you from your tragic revision prison. The least you can do is get me…" KT looked around, licking her lips — her eyes landed on a 'Hook-a-Duck' stall covered with soft-toy prizes, "… a teddy!"

"But…"

"You won't even have to nick it! Watch!"

KT undid another shirt button so the white lace of her bra was on show. Then she smeared some cherry-red lip gloss over her mouth and grabbed Molly's phone.

"Hey, mister, will you take a photo of us?"

The guy behind the stall was late twenties, with yellowing teeth, stubble and acne all over his chin. Tattoos covered his scrawny arms.

"All right, love," he leered, his eyes slipping over KT's body.

Molly watched — fascinated and horrified — as KT flirted with the guy — Gaz — laughing at his pathetic jokes, running a hand over his tattoos and squealing, "Wow! You're all muscle!"

He gave her a teddy bear.

Molly started to feel sick.

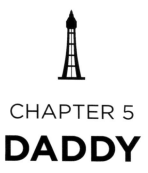

CHAPTER 5
DADDY

The sun was moving down towards the horizon, bringing with it a new chill in the air.

"I need to get home," Molly said. "I told Dad I'd make supper."

KT raised an eyebrow and sucked on the giant, red sugar dummy. "Whatever," she muttered. "I'm going to hang here. Gaz said some of the boys are going to the beach later."

Molly shivered. It was cold outside the sunshine of KT's attention.

"Better hurry home to Daddy!"

Molly was stung by the sarcasm in KT's voice. "It's not that. He…"

But KT had turned away. She was leaning towards Gaz and giggling. The evening lights were flickering on now, giving the Pleasure Beach an odd, dreamy light.

"Maybe see you again sometime," said Molly.

"Maybe," said KT. But she didn't turn around.

Molly made her way back through the backstreets, wishing she'd brought a hoodie. It was too late to go back to the launderette. And she didn't have money to pay, anyway. There was no money for supper either, but when she got home she saw the lights were off.

"Dad?" She pushed open the front door.

In the dark sitting-room her father still sat in the same chair. Asleep now, a can of beer in one hand. Molly turned off the flickering TV set, pulled a blanket off the sofa and laid it carefully over him.

Then she climbed into bed, feeling hungry and sick now. In the gloom she could still make out the revision timetable above her desk. She had only lost one day. She'd get back on track tomorrow. And the break had probably done her good.

All work and no play makes Molly a dull, dull girl.

Right?

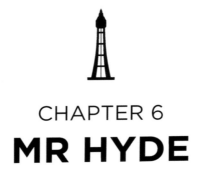

CHAPTER 6
MR HYDE

Molly overslept and the sun was already streaming through the window by the time she awoke. It was going to be the hottest summer on record, the radio was saying as she made hot coffee to shake the heavy feeling in her head.

She tried to focus on English, cramming her brain with quotations from *Dr Jekyll and Mr Hyde*.

"'Man is not truly one but truly two'," she muttered the words for the millionth time, feeling them slide through the gaps in her head. Again.

What did that even mean? She remembered the teacher talking about it in class. Miss Foreman kept her behind afterwards. "Is something bothering you, Molly?" That was before anyone knew about Mum. Afterwards, teachers said, "I understand what you must be going through," then abandoned her on a sea of grief without a life raft.

Her phone beeped. It was another text from Sara. The millionth she'd sent since the funeral.

Molly had known Sara since primary school. Mum said they were like two peas in a pod. Mum had loved Sara.

Hey, Molls. How's it going? My head is stuffed. Fancy a break? Coffee & cake?

Molly pushed away a memory of her and Sara making fairy cakes with Mum, flour all over the kitchen, Mum letting them lick the spoon.

Sorry. Need to revise.

She wanted to add something else but no words came. She pushed the phone aside.

It beeped again.

Shame. Another day?

This time Molly didn't reply.

Dad was up and about this morning. He'd shaved and put on clean clothes, although his shirt was crumpled. Mum had always done the ironing.

"I'm going to the supermarket," he said. "You need some brain food, right?" He was trying to sound like his old self.

"Blueberries and seed mix, please," said Molly.

"That bird food you like to eat?" He laughed.

"It's good for concentration. Mum said so…"

She tailed off. Dad looked awkwardly at his hands. "I'll be back in an hour," he said without meeting her eye. "Don't work too hard. You were up here for hours yesterday."

She paused. If he hadn't even noticed she'd been gone, there was no point telling him now. "Sure, Dad."

And then he was gone and there was a ring on the doorbell.

It was KT.

CHAPTER 7
CHILLAX

"How did you know where I live?"

"You told me, you idiot!" KT stood there grinning. She wore the same pair of ripped jeans, coupled with a crumpled cropped tee, rolled up at the arms to expose a tattoo on her shoulder. The heart locket twinkled at her neck. She looked like she'd slept with her make-up on but the sludgy-eyeliner look was kind of sexy somehow.

"We're going to the beach!" KT announced. "There's loads of other Year 11s. Revision picnic."

"I can't…"

"Don't you read the research, MC? Got to take frequent breaks when revising. And we'll just go for an hour."

Molly noticed the sparkle of a gem in KT's bare midriff that she hadn't seen the day before.

"Did you get your belly pierced?"

"Yeah, yesterday. Don't you remember?"

Molly stared at the red ring around the fake diamond stud. It looked sore and sexy at the same time.

"You should get yours done too," KT said.

"My dad would flip!"

"Would he?" A lazy smile played on KT's face. "Would he actually even notice?"

Molly flushed.

"Look, MC, chillax. Didn't you used to come top of the class in everything?"

It was true, though Molly didn't remember telling KT. Before Mum got ill she'd been the kid who aced every exam. "Probably Oxbridge material," the head had said. But that was before Mum, before she fell behind, before everything went upside down…

"So — you can live a little — take a break. Relax! What can possibly go wrong?"

KT grabbed Molly's hand and looked her straight in the eye.

"And Niall will be there!"

CHAPTER 8
LIP GLOSS

There was a crowd of kids from Molly's year sitting down on the beach. Some of them were drinking cans of cider. There were bags of Doritos and somebody had attached mini speakers to their phone, which was blaring out tunes that chimed tinnily across the sand. None of them looked like they were revising.

Then she spotted Niall.

"You have to talk to him," KT was saying.

Molly's brain was racing. Had she really told KT that she fancied Niall Corey? She had liked him since the day he'd turned round in Geography and asked if she had an ink cartridge — like he'd known that she was the only other person in school who still used a fountain pen. She must have told KT, although she didn't remember it. Maybe her memory was so crammed with information that stuff was starting to fall out.

KT was already making adjustments — tying Molly's baggy T-shirt in a knot above her belly button and smearing lip gloss over her mouth. "We are giving you an instant 'cool-over'!" she declared. "KT equals MC UNsquared!"

She stood back, admiring her handiwork before tugging a mini bottle of whisky out of her back pocket. It was like the ones Dad kept in his bathroom cabinet. The ones he didn't think Molly knew about. Molly started to protest but KT was already unscrewing the bottle.

"Dutch courage," she said, slugging back half and handing the rest to Molly with a look that was hard to refuse.

Molly lifted it reluctantly to her lips. The liquid burned her throat, making her head swim but clearing some of the clammy fear from her stomach.

Then KT was skipping down the beach, pulling Molly along with her, plonking herself down next to Niall and greeting him enthusiastically, like she'd known him for years.

Niall looked confused. He was tall and gangly but he still had a baby face and blonde hair with a stubborn cowlick that he was constantly pushing up from his forehead, as he did now.

"This is Molls!" KT was saying, eyes wickedly bright, lips glistening with strawberry gloss.

Niall smiled awkwardly. "Yup — I know Molly."

Molly felt her cheeks redden.

"So... um... how's the revision going?" Niall asked.

"Seriously, are we really going to talk about exams?" said KT. "The sun is shining. We're young, hot and beautiful. We should be getting drunk and screwing like rabbits. That's what nature intended."

Niall laughed and pushed at his hair nervously. "Yeah… um… I guess you're right."

"Of course I'm right. This should be a summer of sex, drugs and rock'n'roll! Not $E = mc^2$ and all that 'Man is not truly one but truly two' crap."

Niall laughed. "What's that even about? I was trying to figure it out this morning!"

"Have you been revising *Dr Jekyll and Mr Hyde* too?" Molly could feel her cheeks fill with colour.

"Yeah — it's kind of interesting, right? I might even like it if we didn't have to cram our brains full of it!"

Niall smiled and she managed to smile back. Holding his eye made her stomach jump and the whisky seemed to purr in her brain.

"Seriously, the pair of you! This is SO boring!" KT jumped up and headed off down the beach. "See you later, exam-dorks!"

CHAPTER 9
WAVES

They watched her go, spinning barefoot over the pebbles towards the dull grey surf.

"So, revision sucks, doesn't it!" Niall said eventually.

"The more I try to cram in my head, the more I feel falling out!" Molly admitted.

"Me too!" he laughed. Then, after a moment he looked at her again and added, "I'm glad you came."

He held her eye a beat longer this time. Molly felt another bolt of fear and excitement shoot through her.

"Anyone for a swim?"

Molly turned to see KT on the edge of the waves. The freezing brown sludge of the Irish Sea would be sub-zero at this time of year. But KT was laughing as she flung herself forwards into the breakers then surfacing, wet and sparkling in the summer sunshine.

Niall was transfixed by KT. And no wonder: KT's face was alive, her hair dripping, T-shirt clinging so tight to her chest you could see everything.

"She's cool, right?" said Molly.

Niall, an odd intense look on his face, stared at KT shimmying in the waves, light sparkling across her bare skin.

He definitely wasn't thinking about Jekyll and Hyde any more and he seemed to have forgotten Molly even existed. But then who could blame him — who would be in interested in MC^2 while KT was round?

She stood up to leave, and that's when she caught sight of Sara. She was with Rhian and Immy, old mates of theirs from primary school days, up on the promenade, and they were laughing at something on Rhian's phone.

Then Sara looked around. KT's screeches must have caught her attention and she turned towards the beach. She saw Molly and for a split second started to smile, but then she stopped.

A puzzled, hurt expression crossed her face.

Then she turned quickly away.

CHAPTER 10
BETRAYAL

KT texted over and over the next day but Molly ignored her. She needed to focus on revising. She couldn't afford to lose another day. Every time the phone beeped she hoped it might be from Sara (who hadn't texted since spotting Molly on the beach), or even from Niall (though he probably didn't even know her surname, let alone her number), but it was KT. Again and again.

Why u ignorin me?

Whassup, MC???

Molly had left the beach soon after KT emerged from the ocean and demanded Niall lend her his hoodie to warm her up. Molly's last image as she trudged back up the shingle was of KT tugging Niall's arm around her shoulder, saying, "You know the best way to keep warm is if we both strip naked and share body heat."

Another text: *Did I do something 2 upset u?*

Molly flung the phone aside. If Niall wasn't interested in her that was fine. It was KT's betrayal that hurt most.

She picked up a pile of Physics notes and tried to read the numbers and letters that danced before her eyes.

"How many times do I need to say I'm sorry?"

Molly looked up to see KT's grinning face at the window, her body perched half-in, half-out.

"KT, how on earth did you get up here?"

"Climbed on your shed roof, didn't I?" KT was laughing as Molly helped her clamber over the windowsill. "Like you said you used to do when you were a kid!"

KT's eyes were bright as she surveyed the room — almost like she was high, or drunk. She smelled of cheap perfume and peach schnapps. Like Mum used to drink.

"What are you doing here?"

"You wouldn't answer my texts." KT shrugged.

"'Cos I need to work."

KT went over to the mantelpiece, picking up the nick-nacks — a shell from the beach, a crystal dog, a picture of Mum before she lost her hair.

"Look, nothing happened with your precious Niall, OK?" KT said. "We talked about you, mostly. And exams. He's as bad as you with all this revision!"

Then KT was picking up Molly's beautifully coloured revision plan.

"In fact, he was asking if you were coming to this party tonight. Under the pier."

"I can't…"

KT still had hold of the revision schedule, and she was staring at Molly. Her eyes dangerously bright suddenly.

"Does your dad have any booze we can nick?"

"What?"

"Or we could take some of your mum's Malibu or Blue Bols. You said he never drinks that stuff 'cos it tastes of her."

"KT, seriously!"

"What you gonna wear?" KT was tugging Molly's wardrobe open, pulling clothes out, throwing them on the floor. "I was thinking we could crop those skanky jeans of yours. Turn them into itty-bitty shorts. Niall won't be able to resist."

"Why are you even doing this?" Molly asked. "Why are you bothering with me?"

KT shrugged but didn't give an answer.

"Anyway, Dad said he'd cook dinner," Molly said. "So I can't…"

"Will he, though?" asked KT, spinning around again, surveying the piles of notes laid out on Molly's bed, neat stacks of revision cards, post-it notes, practice papers. "Did he even make it to the supermarket yesterday or did he end up in the pub?"

Molly felt a momentary flash of anger then a sick thud in her stomach. Because KT was right.

"You need to forget all this!" said KT, picking up one of the Physics sheets, scrunching it up into a ball and chucking it onto the floor.

"KT!" Molly protested but KT just laughed and picked up a turquoise folder of notes. English. All

Molly's carefully written-out *Dr Jekyll and Mr Hyde* quotations, all her notes, all her essays.

KT's face was gleeful. "No notes, no stress, right?"

"KT, stop messing around!"

But KT was dancing down the stairs now, two steps at a time, the folder in her arms. "Your notes are going to the party. You're coming too, Molly!"

CHAPTER 11
UNSQUARED

Molly didn't think KT would actually do it. She figured it was just a way to get her to come out.

"Come on, give it back!"

KT stood at the end of the pier, hair blowing in the wind off the sea. They sky was scarily dark and there was a damp chill in the air that didn't feel like summer.

"I'm doing you a favour." KT was laughing as she tugged pages out of the revision folder, letting them fly on the wind. Molly watched her notes fall to the dark waves below.

"You want Niall to notice you, you gotta get your nose out of your books," KT was saying. She had a bottle of Mum's Blue Bols and she took a swig from it, then declared, "Your head's so messed up you're probably gonna fail anyway, MC!"

"I am not!"

Molly lunged forwards, swiping at the folder in KT's hands. They were at the edge of the pier now, and she could see the water swirling below. For a second Molly felt an overwhelming impulse to push KT off the edge.

Why was KT doing this?

Why was she doing any of this?

But then KT let go of the folder, shoving it roughly into Molly's arms.

"Fine!" she said, dancing out of the way, mouth laughing, eyes sparkling dangerously. "God, you are SO boring, MC. So totally square!"

Then she turned away, hips swinging, hands raised in the air. "Don't say I didn't try to unsquare you!"

CHAPTER 12
JEALOUS

"Are you OK?"

It was Sara, standing a few metres away, staring at her with a concerned face.

Molly was still clutching the folder, still staring into the space where KT had been. How long had she been standing there?

"I'm… fine," she answered stiffly.

"I saw what just happened. I… you…"

A few of the other girls from school were over

by the arcade. Sara must have come with them. They were giggling about something, glancing in Molly's direction.

Molly felt sick, dizzy.

"I'm just getting a breath of fresh air," she said, her own voice sounding weirdly distant. "All work and no play makes Molly a dull girl, right?" She laughed.

"Right." Sara stared at her with an expression Molly couldn't make out. "Look, I'm here with Rhian and some of the girls if you... want to join us. We're just going for pizza."

"I'm going to a party," Molly said, aware she was speaking too loud, too fake. Not like herself.

"Sure." Sara looked as if she was about to go, then she said, "Molls — when I saw you, yesterday... I mean, that girl," she hesitated, "... it just doesn't seem like you. I hardly recognise you any more."

Molly felt suddenly as if she might cry. She'd tried so hard not to cry in front of Sara. In front of anyone. And Sara was looking at her with pity in her eyes that made Molly feel like screaming.

"I'm just having fun," she said tightly. "No need for you to get all jealous…"

A spasm of pain seemed to cross Sara's face. Then something else. But she shrugged and said, "OK, but if you change your mind…"

"I won't!"

"Fine." Sara waited — just for a beat — then added, "But be careful, Molls."

CHAPTER 13
DRINK

She hacked off the legs of her jeans with a pair of scissors in the grimy pier toilets, ditching the half-empty turquoise folder in a trash can. The Blue Bols that KT had left behind tasted disgusting, but it made her head buzz excitedly and washed away the aftertaste of the conversation with Sara.

By the time Molly had made her way to the West Pier it was dark and her limbs were tingling with alcohol and cold. The party was happening under the pier, where water dripped onto rusty-smelling pebbles and the smell of seaweed mingled with that of stale urine and cigarette smoke. KT was nowhere to be seen and Molly didn't recognise most of the people. Someone had lit a large bonfire and music blasted out of an old-fashioned looking speaker system.

"All right, darling!" A voice loomed towards her out of the darkness. It was Gaz, the stallholder from the Pleasure Beach. The one who'd given KT the teddy. He was grabbing her arm, his breath reeking of alcohol. Molly shook him off.

"Hey — leave her alone." Molly turned, wishing suddenly that her head wasn't so fuzzy as she found herself face to face with Niall.

"Glad you came," he said. "You look…" he hesitated, fumbled with his hair, "um… great."

She wasn't sure why but she reached out and touched his arm. The way she'd seen KT do to Gaz.

"So do you!" she heard herself saying. "Have you been working out?"

"Um… no." Niall frowned. He was looking at her oddly now.

"Would you get me a drink?" She tried to say it how KT had — at the Pleasure Beach — making the request sound like a promise.

"Yeah… um… sure." Niall moved away and Molly closed her eyes to try and steady the buzzing in her brain.

Then she opened them again.

And saw KT.

CHAPTER 14
KISSING

"You need to make him jealous!"

"What?"

"He thinks you're acting weird!"

"I know, but…"

"Show him other guys want you then he'll want you too."

KT was wearing a tiny pair of cut-off shorts and a strappy vest. Goose pimples marked her bare flesh and made the tattoo on her shoulder look like a red grimace but she didn't seem to notice.

"Just follow my lead, OK!"

Then KT was grabbing Gaz and kissing him full on the lips. Molly watched in a mixture of horror and fascination as KT ground her body against him. Gaz's hands were all over KT.

Molly felt herself stumble sideways, her vision swimming. And then there was Niall, with two bottles of beer in his hands. Motionless, staring transfixed. Just like when KT did her 'Miss Wet T-shirt' act.

"Your turn," said KT, coming up for air. Her eyelids were oddly droopy, her lip gloss smeared all around her mouth.

Gaz was grinning at Molly now in a way that made her feel naked. KT handed her the nearly empty bottle of Blue Bols. Her tongue was turquoise — the colour of Molly's English folder. Molly took a slug, the liquorice taste thick and disgusting on her tongue.

Then she turned to Gaz. "Good girls can party too!" she said, loud enough for Niall to hear.

And then his lips were on hers and his breath smelled of stale beer and fags, and his hands were rough on her skin but she pressed herself closer, blocking out the rising tide of nausea.

And then she was pulling away from him, stumbling, grabbing one of his friends. "Want to share?" she heard herself say. And then she was kissing the other guy — he was much older, with a paunch and stubble that was coarse against her face.

And then someone was pulling her off. "Molls — stop!"

She swung round to see Sara. Only her face seemed to be swimming. Lurching through the air. Molly shook her off.

"Aren't I even allowed to have any fun?" Her voice was unnaturally loud against the roar of the waves and the blare of the music. "It's not like anyone died… Oh — oops!"

And then she was laughing and laughing and Sara was backing away, looking disgusted.

And that's when she saw KT kissing Niall.

CHAPTER 15
EQUATIONS

She went mad then. A broken bottle of Blue Bols was in her hand — she was vaguely aware of having smashed it against the iron girder of the pier — and there was blood running down her fingers. And everyone was looking at her, but not how she wanted them to look. Not how they looked at KT. But with the look of pity that she'd seen in everyone's eyes since Mum had been diagnosed. The look she'd been avoiding. The reason she hadn't wanted to see Sara. Because that pity-look made her feel sick and small and scared all at once.

And now she was drunk too, so drunk that words and quotes and equations spilled out of her head into the dark night air.

$$E = mc^2$$

Man is not truly one but truly two

Faces were looming all around, glaring, staring so it felt like she was in a house of mirrors, turning frantically, seeing distorted reflections of herself wherever she looked.

"Give me the bottle, Molls!" Sara was saying.

And Niall too. Pity in his eyes. "Molls — let go of the bottle."

No sign of KT.

And then she took the sharp-ended bottle and plunged it into her own arm.

CHAPTER 16
BLUR

She woke up in a hospital bed.

The room was bright. Sunshine flooded the window. Sara and Niall sat on chairs by the bed. No sign of KT. No sign of Dad.

Sara told her she was going to be OK. "You had your stomach pumped," she said gently.

"And your arm has been stitched up," Niall added, his face flushed, his hair a crumpled mess.

Molly glanced down at the bandages on her wrist, remembering the sharp pain of the bottle, the blissful darkness just before she hit the wet pebbles.

"Where's Dad?" she croaked. Her throat felt tight, scratchy.

"He's been here all night," said Sara. "He just popped out for a few moments — said something about meeting the washing-machine man. He'll be back though. He bought you blueberries and those funny seeds you like."

Molly glanced at the food on the side-table. She couldn't imagine ever being hungry again.

"What about KT?"

The memories from the previous night were a hazy blur but she remembered KT dancing, KT kissing Niall, KT at the end of the pier, throwing her notes into the sea.

"Has she been to see me?"

Sara and Niall exchanged a look. "You've been under loads of pressure, Molly-Cate —" Sara started to say.

Molly looked up. Only her oldest friend still called her by her full name.

Molly.

Cate.

With a hyphen.

"KT, has she been to see me?" she asked again.

"You kept asking for her," Niall started to say. "And the doctors said —"

"Hasn't she even texted?" Molly could feel panic rising in her chest. Her throat was agony, her head throbbing, her limbs felt like lead. She fumbled for her phone and frantically searched her texts. There was nothing from KT.

Nothing.

And all her previous texts had been erased.

She'd even been deleted from Molly's contacts.

"Did you delete her?" she demanded, filled suddenly with a dizzying sense of sickness and anger. Anger like she'd felt at the end of the pier, when she'd been staring down at the water, KT's laughing eyes on hers.

Then she caught sight of her reflection in the mirror on the opposite wall. The sunken eyes, the bleeding lip gloss, smudges of eyeliner… the heart-shaped locket around her neck.

Molly.

Cate.

MC^2.

"You kept asking for KT," Niall said again. "The doctors were asking who she was. Nobody knew…"

Molly could see but not feel the tears filling her eyes as she stared and stared at her own reflection. "But you knew…"

"The doctor says it's all the stress you've been under," Sara was saying. Her voice was gentle, careful. "And the trauma of your mum's death."

"But you saw her," she turned to Niall. "On the beach — running in the waves. You kissed her."

But he was just looking at her and she could see herself reflected double — one in each of his concerned brown eyes.

"The doctor said that kind of thing can be the trigger for a kind of psychotic breakdown…" Sara was saying.

"No!" Molly turned away from the double images of herself, looked frantically at Sara. "You were there too. You know she was real."

"They call it dissociative identity disorder," Niall was saying. His face was red, the words came out slowly, awkwardly. "It happened to a cousin of mine…"

Molly turned back to the mirror, memories rewriting themselves in her brain. Switching perspective like a mirror image, or a selfie, where everything is reversed, turned around, seen from a different angle.

Her reflection in the glass of the washing machine. *Her* hands full of revision notes throwing them into the sea. The voice in her own head saying: *All work and no play makes Molly a dull girl.*

Man is not truly one but truly two

$KT = MC^2$.

Molly-Cate.

MC.

KT.

"Are you saying… she wasn't real?"

Sara didn't answer.

"And the stuff she did…" Molly stared at her oldest friend as the full truth dawned, "I did?"

Neither Sara nor Niall could quite meet her eye.

Running in the water, flirting with the guys at the Pleasure Beach, throwing her notes to the winds, kissing those men — throwing herself at Niall. Had it all been her?

"I… she…"

"The doctors say you're going to be fine," said Sara softly.

"You probably get to skip exams too!" said Niall with an awkward smile. "If you want to."

Molly turned to stare out of the window, desperately blinking back tears. From here you could just see the curve of the Big Dipper wheeling over the Pleasure Beach, Blackpool Tower and the sea beyond. They all looked murky through the tears pooling in her eyes. She didn't know what she wanted. Or how she felt. Humiliated. Frightened. Confused.

Lonely.

Without KT she felt suddenly horribly alone.

"I miss her," she said. She wasn't sure if she meant Mum or KT. Or some version of herself she'd lost with both of them.

"I know," said Sara.

"But she'll always be — I dunno — part of you," said Niall.

He looked awkward, uncomfortable, pushing back his hair with the familiar nervous motion. And Molly wondered why he had stayed. Why Sara had stayed. Who had they stayed for?

It wasn't for KT. Because KT wasn't real.

And then she realised they had stayed for her.

For Molly-Cate.

And then she let the tears fall.

ABOUT THE AUTHOR

Catherine Bruton is the author of several critically acclaimed novels for teens and young adults, and has been described as 'one of the finest teen writers of recent years' (*The Guardian*). Her debut novel *We Can be Heroes* was recently adapted into a film starring Alison Steadman and Phil Davies. Later titles include *Pop!* and the multi-award-nominated *I Predict a Riot*. Catherine lives in Bath with her husband and two children, and teaches English part-time at King Edward's School.